Mom & Dad Got Us a Baby

Written by Katelyn Hoglund
Illustrated by Abby Nurre

MOM & DAD GOT US A BABY

PALMETTO
PUBLISHING
Charleston, SC
www.PalmettoPublishing.com

Mom & Dad Got Us a Baby
Copyright © 2023 by Katelyn Hoglund

First Edition

Hardcover ISBN: 979-8-8229-0840-6
Paperback ISBN: 979-8-8229-0841-3
eBook ISBN: 979-8-8229-0842-0

This book is dedicated to all of the dogs
waiting for us at the Rainbow Bridge, the
new ones who will come into our lives, and
to all of the babies who share a speical bond with their
animal companions.

To my Mom and Dad: Thank you for raising me to know the
love of a dog in our childhood home - and for doing most of the
work. More importantly, thank you for never giving up on me.

To my husband, Jeffrey: Thank you for letting me have so many
dogs. I'm glad you convinced me that kids are kind of cool, too.
Being on this journey with you has been
my own personal Eighth Wonder of
the World.

To my children, Ellianna and Collier:
Thank you for giving me purpose and a
fun story to write. I'm glad we didn't have
to rehome either of you due to dog allergies.

To my dogs, past and present:
Thank you for existing.

In memory of Jack who mosied across
the Rainbow Bridge during the
publication of this book.

Mom and Dad got us a baby
And now we're not so sure

If our happy home will still be sweet
And comfy and secure.

Will baby take all the attention,
Leaving us out in the cold?

Will our snacks completely vanish?
Will Mom just serve a scold?

And Mom and Dad
Did you forget?
Babies will bite!
Babies will hit!

They storm and stomp.
They throw their toys.
We don't think we
Can stand the noise!

We worry we won't get to stay
In our place right by your side.

We think instead we'll have to find
A safe spot where we can hide!

Our greatest fear, we must confess,
The real doom that we dread:

Will your heart still hold your love for us
Or only for baby instead?

Listen up, you silly pups,
Is Mom's laughing reply.
You'll still be kept within my heart
And I'll tell the reason why.

You've been fit inside that space;
My heart will always hold you!
I'll never run out of room to love
My sweet and furry crew.

The perk of a growing family
Is a growing love as well.

The more we multiply our pack,
The more our hearts will swell.

Don't you worry, my darling dogs,
And believe me when I say,
No matter who comes in that's new,
You're in my heart to stay.

The baby will grow to love you, too!
She'll give nice pats and sweet hugs.

We'll teach her not to give hard smacks.
We'll say "no" to hurtful tail-tugs.

And soon enough it's time for snacks
When baby will want to share.
Kilo better stay nearby
To snatch treats from the air.

Now, thinks Jack, it's a good thing
That Mom has a big enough lap:
One knee for the baby
And one knee for this chap!

And next we'll need all your help
When our girl's in the bath.
Some bubbles with her Kain-Bub
Will make our baby laugh.

It's time to read a storybook,
So let's learn how to snuggle.

Sally, come on! Jump up here!
And give us your best nuzzle.

At last, there's the cozy crib,
Where baby says goodnight.
But not before a Lotto-hug
In the glowing moon's soft light.

Now, dear Mom, your puppies see
And so we won't be sad.
We understand that this new life
Can't be all that bad.

We'll like one more person to sniff and to lick,
One more face to greet at our door,
One more set of hands to pet our soft fur,
One more creature to kiss and adore.

We believe your promise to keep your heart true
And to love us as much as before.
Welcome to our pack, Ellianna,
We'll be glad to share love with one more.

Uh-oh!

MEET THE PACK!

Jack - This Great Dane is a true Mama's boy at heart and proclaims it to everyone. He doesn't have time for shenanigans and regularly uses his booming barks to let others know. Small couch? No problem. Jack will just sit in your lap!

Lotto - A true dog's dog, Great Dane Lotto is more like a puppy for the other pups. He gallops through the house bringing with him plenty of laughs and even more slobber. Wherever Lotto is, Kain is trailing close by, always at the ready to mother the much bigger-than-him puppy. If Lotto can't be found, well then it's likely he found trouble...

Kain - found abandoned in a crate as a young puppy, Kain, an American Staffordshire, shares his gratitude for being rescued by giving as many kisses as he can, as often as he can. A Mama in a dog's body, Kain loves and cherishes babies of all species. But, he has an affinity for toilet paper rolls, so keep yours guarded at all costs.

Kilo - Dubbed The Fun Police during her reign, American Staffordshire Kilo enjoyed the quiet, solo life. She didn't like getting tangled up in dog drama and much preferred being with her people, mainly her Dad. Kilo had a mind of her own. Like clockwork every night, she would meander to the bottom of the stairs to give us a stern, "Boof, boof, boof, it's time to go up!" when bedtime was near.

Sally - Though she doesn't look much like one, the Boxer in her comes out when she shows her love! She's also part affectionate American Staffordshire, which explains why she is always nearby. You will hear her tail thumping long before someone walks in the door. But be careful! She will wiggle her way into your heart while simultaneously nibbling the jewelry off your earlobes!

Yahtzee - While this floppy and funny Great Dane puppy was only with us for a short time, she brought immense joy to our lives during especially challenging months. Yahtzee showed us that silver linings exist in all situations.

About the Author

Katelyn Hoglund is a wife, mother, content creator, author, inspirational leader, and dog rescue advocate. As a lover of celebrating both the big and small moments of life, she is best known for videos of her dogs' birthday parties, her blog about the many lessons she has learned on this journey through life, and her family's antics on Facebook. Katelyn and her husband, Jeffrey, enjoy an always-full house and stay on their toes with two children, Ellianna and Collier, and their ever changing pack of dogs. They look forward to and welcome each new day of chaos. As Katelyn likes to say, it's not a coincidence that dog is God spelled backwards. Thank you God, for giving us dogs.

Milton Keynes UK
Ingram Content Group UK Ltd.
UKHW050922230824
447218UK00008B/49